The Haunting of I

CW00431587

©2018 by Carrie Bates

Prologue

November 28, 1915, Providence

Wyatt Harper had lived in the same house his entire life. It sat isolated and somewhat unkempt in the suburbs of Providence. It was tucked away behind the thorny branches and overgrowth. The trek to and from civilization was no easy feat. The road to the Harper House was a winding snake. Nobody, save for Wyatt, lived amongst the trees and the forest creatures. For this reason, the path was not maintained. It wound wild through the forest, going on for as far as the eye could see.

The feeble man trudged tediously along the beaten dirt road. His knuckles were white and wrapped around the handle of a large leather physician's bag. The contents of this bag were both precious and potent; he couldn't allow the bitter wind to snatch them from his grasp. Perhaps the most precious of them was a bottle of rose-scented humectant. Wyatt hugged this bottle close to his body. He didn't trust it clattering around with the other bottles in the bag.

Mabel needed a new color. She needed a new scent. That nice mercantile at the mortuary supply shop had all the fixings Wyatt required for his beloved Mabel. The rose scented humectant he sold Wyatt would rejuvenate his Mabel's soft milky skin and add girth to her poor wilted temples. Wyatt groaned. The bag felt as though it was filled with something far heavier than a couple glass bottles of fluid. The struggle would fare well for Wyatt. This he knew, for he had been desiring his Mabel for days. In her current state, he could not touch her. The bugs were beginning to make friends with her fingers, and her odor was becoming something less pleasant than roses.

"Nothing worth doing is ever easy." Wyatt heard his father's voice drift amongst the whispering tree branches. An amorous man who would overcome any obstacle for the right woman, Levi Harper built the Harper house for his wife, Faith, and son, Wyatt. He, perhaps, had the help of a few contractors, but, even so, Levi was a brilliant craftsman, creator, and caregiver. There had always been money in the family, and so, Levi, Faith, and Wyatt took to a simple life in the woods. They were never ones for flashing their wealth. Faith was an educated woman and taught Wyatt how to read and write. Levi took Wyatt into the forest to hunt wild turkeys and taught him how to grow fruit, vegetables, and herbs.

Life was leisure—life was good… that is, until the accident.

Like any proper family, the Harpers occasionally felt the need to leave their house. Although they valued their privacy, they also valued their sanity. Becoming a total social recluse never did a man's mind justice. For this reason, the Harpers kept a horse and buggy and would use it to travel into Providence. Unfortunately for the Harpers, their horse suffered a mental break. Wyatt was twenty years of age during the episode. He and his mother sat comfy in the back of the buggy whilst his father played coachman. All of a sudden, their horse began to scream and buck. It was as though the poor creature had become possessed. The Harpers were thrown from their buggy. Levi tumbled head first into a knotted tree root, breaking his neck and dying instantly. Faith managed to survive the fall, but was clobbered to death by the deranged horse's hooves. Suddenly, Wyatt was an orphan.

The funeral proceedings that followed were both agonizing and inspiring for Wyatt. His parents were killed abruptly by their own horse. It was the sort of tragedy that lived in his veins, filling his entire body with misery. The only silver lining was Wyatt's vocation. After the deaths of his parents, Wyatt was forced to find an undertaker to prepare their bodies. Though beaten and bruised leading up to their demise, the bodies of Wyatt's parents appeared at peace for their funerals. Wyatt decided, upon seeing the embalmed bodies of his parents, that he wanted to learn the art of embalming for himself.

Wyatt chuckled just then. "That's when I met my marvelous Mabel!" he exclaimed. The memory brought him great joy.

He'd first laid eyes on her during a viewing at her home. Mabel's family had just moved from the south to Providence. During their trip, Mabel's younger sister, Esther, contracted scarlet fever. She died shortly after their arrival, and was positioned doll-like in her bed. Wyatt had been so proud of the restoration work he'd done on Esther. No more were her dehydrated eyes and shriveled features. Esther looked a sleeping beauty surrounded with flowers and dressed in lace. Mabel, on the other hand, resembled a ghost. Her features were profoundly pale. Her hair blazed red and was a stark contrast against her fair skin. When she spoke, her voice floated softly through the air like the wind on the first days of summer. Her eyes were wide and watery, and her lips always seemed to be trembling. She was magically morose. The two fell madly in love. Having been so deprived of affection for so long, Wyatt's passion was fervent. Mabel was just as keen a lover as Wyatt, and the two lived happily in the Harper House for some time.

A year had passed since their wedding when Wyatt discovered he was going to be a father. He'd desperately hoped for a son he could name after his father. A daughter would have done splendidly as well, for he could name her after his mother. Either way, Wyatt loved his child before it was conceived.

The pain washed over Wyatt all at once. His body and mind seemed to be aching in synchronicity. His heart hammered and his breath escaped him.

"Time for a break," he muttered to himself. He carefully placed the bag and humectant on the dirt road and stretched his bemoaning arms over his head. He would do anything to have both his Mabel and his Junior. Wyatt had attempted to save Junior the way he saved Mabel, but the procedure was difficult to complete with an infant-sized frame. Wyatt moaned and sunk to his knees. "My poor Junior!" he lamented.

The night of Mabel's delivery had been a stormy one. The rain hammered the windows of the Harper House while thunder and lightning prefaced one another in the distance. Wyatt remembered the dampness of Mabel's hand as she agonized in labor. He stayed with her the entire time, sweeping her hair from her face and whispering words of encouragement. He'd done everything he could to support her during her pregnancy, including resigning from his embalming job. Wyatt's time belonged to Mabel; she was his life.

Even with the aid of an obstetric physician, Mabel's delivery went far from smoothly. She lost far too much blood far too quickly. At one point, the baby's head surfaced, but the remainder of its body was still inside the birthing canal. The physician explained that the baby's shoulder was caught on the pelvis, thus rendering it stuck and unable to receive oxygen. Mabel's body had long gone still. Wyatt prayed she'd merely lose consciousness. When the physician finally managed to free the baby, it was blue.

"I'm sorry, Mr. Harper, but your wife and son did not survive." The physician's voice would forever haunt Wyatt.

"You're wrong!" Wyatt declared, taking up the bag and humectant once more. "My Mabel is still alive and still as beautiful to me as ever!" With a new found determination, Wyatt continued his trek through the tumultuous night.

As the years went by, Wyatt grew more and more reclusive. His mind dissolved in his skull like smoke, away from anyone to notice. He had no friends to assist him in his grief, and his closest neighbor lived a mile away. He lived off of fried grubs and weeds, refusing to go into town for supplies. The only time the people of Providence noticed Wyatt's presence was when he visited the mortuary supply shop. Wyatt frequented the shop on a biweekly basis. The mercantile wasn't one to ask questions. Who was he to deter business? On a number of occasions, Wyatt was stopped on the streets and questioned. If he wasn't in the funeral industry anymore, what was he doing with bags full of embalming fluid? Wyatt claimed he needed them for anatomical research purposes. It wasn't a total lie…

"After all, I research Mabel's anatomy on a daily basis!" Wyatt cackled. He would have to tell that joke to Mabel later.

At long last, Wyatt could see the tarnished shingles of the house's roof from between the lace-like branches of the trees. The house was not as welcoming as it once was. What had once been the stable for the horse and buggy was now a lopsided sagging structure coated in decaying leaves and dirt. The color of the house was disguised in gray. Areas of the roof had turned concave. The evident flaws in the house were not visible to Wyatt's eyes. He'd long ago lost the ability to see the real world as it truly was. Instead, he lived in an altered state of reality: a state where madmen dwell.

"Oh, Mabel, I'm home!" Wyatt called. The door creaked eerily as he pressed his weight against it.

The door no longer locked, though, it was hardly necessary given the isolated location of the house. It was unlikely that any burglar would care for anything from such a woebegone structure, anyhow. Nothing inside or outside of the house was cared for, aside from Mabel. It was fortunate that Wyatt's frame was as slight as it was, else he'd surely fall through the moldy wood of the staircase on his way up to see Mabel.

"Wait until you see the special drink I bought for you, Mabel." Wyatt covered his nose and mouth with a handkerchief as he arrived on the second floor of the house. The putridity of the smell was overwhelming. "Nothing a little rose-scented humectant can't fix," he stated. Using the remainder of his waning strength, Wyatt undressed and transferred Mabel's pale, emaciated body to the bathroom and into the bathtub.

"Sorry the water couldn't be warmer, Dear," he said, dowsing her body with water he'd fetched from the well earlier that day. "The cool water is less harsh on your delicate skin." He removed the bottle of rose-scented humectant from the bag and began using the pleasantly odored solution to shampoo her hair.

"Now, Mabel, I can't use all of this delightful humectant on your hair. I have to save some to add girth to your body. You poor thing! You've lost so much weight!" Wyatt cooed over his Mabel, washing her gently and thoroughly. He then dried her tenderly with a sheet and carried her back to bed. He dressed her in her most beautiful white satin night slip and freshened up her makeup before preparing for bed himself.

Exhausted, he slipped under the covers next to her. His old body was arthritic and nutrient deprived. Wyatt's obsession with Mabel consumed his entire life. He rarely ate or drank, and the only time he left his property was to visit the mercantile at the mortuary supply shop. A pain shot down Wyatt's arm. He groaned as he turned towards Mabel.

"So, my dear," he began, caressing her cheek, "you never said, how was your day?" He lay beside her, admiring her red lipstick and rosy cheeks. He breathed in her rose scent, relishing it.

Her soft voice tickled his ear. "I waited so patiently for you. It's been so long since we were last intimate."

"Oh, my darling, I know!" Wyatt exclaimed. "I've desired you for so long. But, you know I had to treat your skin. It's gotten so fragile, and you've lost so much weight! Tomorrow, I'll rejuvenate your body. I'll never leave you, Mabel."

"Oh, Wyatt!" Mabel gasped. "Won't you at least kiss me?"

"Of course, my dear! You know I love you." Wyatt lifted Mabel's head from the pillow. He stroked her hair and kissed her firmly on the lips. As he did so, he felt a constriction in his chest. "Oh!" he gasped, suddenly breathless, "you've really got my heart going, Mabel!" The pain intensified. Wyatt clutched his chest, sweat brewing on his forehead. "Mabel! Help! I—" Wyatt choked on his last breath before going limp.

Chapter One

March 25, 2018, Providence

Blake took a sharp right onto the narrow dirt road. It was a mucky March day, and the dirt road turned like putty beneath the tires of her Jeep. It felt good to be starting fresh. Blake had spent her last three years working in and out of the funeral industry in Canada. She was 22—a young age to be moving to a different country on her own. There had been many ups and downs in her career thus far. She may be young, but she was ready for a greater responsibility than what her previous employers were willing to give her. An opportunity arose for her to work as a prep room manager at a funeral home in Providence. No way could she turn that down! Blake specialized in the restorative arts and had always wanted more control over the happenings in an embalming room. She was tired of holding back—of allowing her higher ups to run disorganized in the prep room, misplacing important documents, refusing to clean and disinfect their instruments—it was time for Blake to assert herself.

Blake didn't particularly care for the hustle and bustle of city life. She was an independent individual and proud of it. That being stated, she did occasionally feel lonely, especially when enveloped in a sea of strangers. For that reason, she made a down payment on a reasonably sized Victorian style house situated about thirty minutes outside of the city in a rather secluded area. Blake didn't know much about the history of the house other than it had been rebuilt several times since its original construction in the 1850s.

"God, this road goes on forever!" she exclaimed. The road twisted back and forth through the dense woods. Bored and desperate for a smoke, Blake reached behind her ear to retrieve the one cigarette she'd been saving for the day. She'd been trying to quit since she started and had managed to cut back to one or two cigarettes a day. She placed the cigarette between her lips, taking her eyes off the road for a moment to light it. She puffed on it and directed her eyes back to the road just in time to see the deer step out in front of her Jeep.

"Oh, God!" she shouted, slamming her foot on the brake. The Jeep lurched and came to a stop just inches away from the creature. The deer blinked nonchalantly. It twitched its ear and snorted. "Get out of the way!" Blake honked the horn. Startled, the deer leapt from the path into the woods, crashing through the twigs and leaves.

"Dang it!" Blake swore. Her heart had practically jumped out of her mouth! Her cigarette had fallen from her lips, extinguishing on the damp car mat. "Just for that I'm going to have to smoke two cigarettes today!" Before continuing on her way, Blake rummaged through her purse for another cigarette. She lit it and inhaled the smoke for a moment before placing the car in drive.

The remainder of her drive was uneventful. She drove past her neighbor's house, which was a mile away from her own, and came to a halt in front of an opening in the forest marked by a wooden sign nailed to a tree. The sign read, 'Harper House.'

"Home sweet home," Blake said. 'Sweet' was certainly an accurate description for the place. As Blake drove down the driveway leading to the house, she was immediately greeted with the sweet smell of roses. Blake remembered smelling the scent during her initial viewing of the house and thinking it odd that there was no rose garden to produce the scent. She later concluded that the realtor must have sprayed a rose scented freshener about the house in order to make it seem more appealing. Oddly enough, the smell reminded Blake of an embalming chemical she used to help add weight to emaciated bodies.

"Why must everything remind me of embalming?" Blake mused, finishing the last of her cigarette and flicking the butt into a disposable coffee cup.

She stepped out of the Jeep in awe of the fact that the house was hers. The house was a manageable size. It certainly wasn't a mansion, but it was no cramped apartment, either. The house had more of a cottage feel to it. The front of the house had windows positioned in a way that almost made it seem like it had eyes. There was a porch where she could lounge during the warmer days of spring, assuming spring ever decided to come. It wasn't in perfect shape. The white paint coating the house was yellowed and flaking in areas. Blake also remembered seeing a ghastly sunflower wallpaper coating the kitchen walls. Weeds, grass, and other shaggy looking plants grew wild throughout the property. It was, however, the house's flaws that gave it character. Blake was determined to make the house her own. A fresh coat of paint here and there, some modern décor, and perhaps a nice garden around the back would liven the place up.

Blake reached into her coat pocket, eagerly fingering the house's key. Her new job didn't commence for another few weeks, giving her plenty of time to get settled and explore the area. Perhaps she would use her time to strip the kitchen of its repulsive flower paper. A lively shade of canary yellow would be a suitable replacement color.

"At long last I have a place to myself," Blake thought, lighting another cigarette. Her first cigarette hadn't counted as she'd barely gotten her lips around it before the deer incident. Gone were the days of sharing everything with obnoxious roommates. The Harper House belonged to Blake.

Chapter Two

The house provided a simple layout. The front
door opened up directly into a room suitable for
lounging or entertaining. To the right of this
room was the kitchen in all its ghastly floral
wonder. At the back of the house was a narrow
set of stairs that led down to a basement storage
area. A bathroom existed off of the kitchen; it
resembled a closet in terms of its size.
Thankfully, a second much larger bathroom was
located across from the master bedroom on the
second floor of the house. Blake was currently
slaving over the assembly of her bed frame.
She'd managed to assemble the base of her bed
and had only the headboard left, when a wave of
exhaustion hit her. Leaning the headboard
against the wall, she decided to call it a night.
She placed her mattress and box spring on the

frame of her bed, unpacked her covers and pillows, and crashed.

Her sleep was rock-like. Undisturbed… until a presence slipped under the blankets next to her. Still in a state of half consciousness, Blake felt the dip in the mattress and assumed her cat had leapt onto the bed. She then remembered her cat died over a year ago. Confusion set in as the blankets crinkled, taking on the form of a human body. Someone was lying next to her. Fear mounted in the back of Blake's mind. She attempted to open her eyes, but her eyes refused to open.

"Oh, no!" she panicked. Blake knew exactly what was happening to her: sleep paralysis. Although Blake's brain was awake, her body was not.

A steady breath tickled her ear. What was happening? Was this a nightmare?! Blake tried desperately to will her eyes open. *"Please wake up! Please wake up!"* Blake begged her body to cooperate. It was then that she experienced something truly unnerving. Cold fingers stroked her cheeks, caressing her face in a fashion that would preclude intimacy. Disturbed, Blake's body finally obeyed. Her eyes shot open, and she immediately began to scream and flail her arms in defense.

"GET AWAY!" she shrieked. "DON'T TOUCH ME!"

Her heart throbbed in her chest. As she settled, she realized she was alone. She took a moment to catch her breath. Then, tentatively, she repositioned herself in bed and fell asleep to the smell of roses.

The sun shone brashly through Blake's bedroom window, causing her to stir at the ungodly hour of 6 am. Blake was not a morning person. She groaned and rolled out of bed, vowing to purchase blackout curtains for the window. Her boxes greeted her with the expectation of being unpacked. They were all there, just as they had been the night before. Blake cringed at the memory of her bizarre nightmare. The idea of someone secretly living in the house with her was unnerving. Blake took a deep breath.

"Relax," she assured herself, *"your stuff is all here, just as it was yesterday. You had a nightmare. Nothing more."* Still anxious, Blake opened the window and inhaled the fresh air. Though refreshing, Blake wasn't calmed by the forest air.

"Screw this!" she muttered. She dug a cigarette from her purse. "I guess I'm having tobacco for breakfast!"

After her breakfast of champions, Blake decided to take a trip into town to pick out a new color for the kitchen. There was a window above the sink that allowed the kitchen to be filled with sunlight. The sun was yellow… why not paint the walls yellow? Perhaps the yellow color of the walls would encourage Blake to feel more alive in the mornings.

Blake's stomach gurgled as she hopped into the jeep. It occurred to her just then that she needed to get groceries while she was out.

"And, don't forget black out curtains!" she reminded herself.

It was hard to believe such a vast and populated city existed just thirty minutes from such an alienated countryside. What Blake admired about the city was its friendly charm. Although it was a proper, sophisticated city, it had the disposition of a humble town.

Blake cursed the fact that she hadn't eaten anything for breakfast. Her stomach groaned and ached for food. So much so, that she pulled into a restaurant for a quick bite to eat. She parked her jeep and exited it, realizing, with a twinge of animosity, that the sun was now nonexistent behind a layer of gray clouds.

"Oh, sure," she thought, *"the sun comes out just in time to wake me from my delicious sleep and then conveniently disappears behind a cloud as soon as I'm up!"* Her somewhat negative thinking was imparted due to her hunger.

Entering the restaurant, she found that it was mostly full of senior citizens. This made sense as seniors tended to be early risers. Blake sat herself in a corner and was immediately greeted by a waiter.

"Hello! Hello! Hello!" the waiter said. He was the sort of guy who wore pants that exposed his ankles, and who wore his loafers barefooted. It was a trendy look for hipster guys who played the guitar. "My name is Clyde. I'll be looking after you today. Can I start you off with anything to drink?"

Blake ordered a spinach and cheese omelet big enough to last her two meals, and, of course, a cup of coffee. As the amiable, bespectacled Clyde returned with her meal, Blake inquired about nearby hardware stores. Clyde recommended some places and asked if she was new to the town.

"Yes, actually," Blake responded. "I just moved to the Harper House yesterday. I'm in the process of redecorating."

Clyde's face lit up just then. "You don't say!" he exclaimed. "My Grandma Mary lives up that way. It's the only other house in that area if I'm not mistaken."

Blake recalled driving past one other house. What a small world. Her happy waiter was her neighbor's grandson!

"Wow. That's a crazy coincidence," Blake said.

"Yeah, it is!" Clyde laughed. His expression suddenly went contemplative. "Now that you mention it, I remember her saying something about the Harper House. Is it… no… was that the house where they found the…" Clyde's face went pink. "Ugh, never mind. My Grandma Mary is a character." He chuckled nervously.

"Enjoy your meal!" He then scuttled away swiftly as though he'd just discovered Blake was a serial killer.

"Well, that was weird," Blake thought. She began adding sugar into her coffee. As she ate her omelet, she replayed Clyde's words over in her head: *'was that the house where they found the...'*

"What?" Blake wondered. *"What did they find?"*

Chapter Three

It was three in the afternoon when Blake returned from her shopping trip. She had four bags of supplies in each hand and struggled to open her front door. She hobbled into the house like a penguin, weighed down with the groceries, paint, and curtains she'd purchased. A grunt of relief escaped her lips as she placed the bags on the floor and stretched her back. She then cracked open a can of soda and collapsed into a wooden dining chair. Although she was glad the house had come furnished, Blake had to admit, the furniture was pretty outdated. She envisioned the dining set painted a sky blue to go with the canary yellow she had chosen for the kitchen walls.

"Perhaps that would be too much color," she thought. "Nah!" she said aloud. It was her house,

she could make it as colorful as she wanted. She chugged the remainder of her soda and then began unpacking her groceries. She figured she'd begin peeling the wallpaper from the kitchen walls and then have an early dinner around 4pm. This way, she'd be giving herself enough time to complete the task before sundown. If she used her time wisely, she might even be able to commence painting tomorrow. It shouldn't take too long to strip the walls of their hideous clothes. The majority of the paper had already begun separating from the walls. All Blake had to do was finish the job.

Blake opened the kitchen cupboards to put away her boxes of pasta, only to find that the cupboards already contained food items. She reached into the cupboard and extracted an ancient can of soup.

"No way!" The label of the can was color blocked red and green. It read: *Crosse and Blackwell Scotch Broth.* She turned the can over in her hands and discovered that it had been manufactured in 1914. Blake laughed. "I've got soup older than my grandma!" She wondered how much antique soup would go for on EBay and made a mental note to do a thorough clean out of all the cupboards.

She finished putting away all of her produce and dried goods, leaving out the bread, a can of tuna, some mayonnaise, and a head of lettuce to make herself some dinner later. It was then that she began attacking the walls.

Blake soon discovered she was kidding herself to think she'd be finished stripping the wallpaper before sundown. Blake wasn't an expert on wallpaper removal and had asked a worker at the hardware store for advice. He'd set her up with all the fixings: a spray bottle, a liquid stripping concentrate, a scraper, a small ladder, and a plastic floor protector.

First, she had to tape the plastic floor protector sheet to her baseboards in order to save on mess. She removed all the loose pieces of wallpaper foremost and then mixed the wallpaper stripping concentrate with warm water in a spray bottle to saturate the wallpaper. What she'd forgotten, was how long the worker had said it would take for the wallpaper to absorb the stripping formula. Blake twiddled her thumbs for thirty minutes before the paper started to budge. Once appropriately absorbed, Blake was able to scrape the paper off in mushy chunks, starting from the highest point of the wall and working her way to the bottom.

Blake looked at her watch and swore. It was ten past four and all she'd managed to remove was a quarter of the paper from one wall. Frustrated, she descended the ladder and went to the counter to fix herself a tuna sandwich.

The can opener clicked into the lid of the can and whirred as Blake turned the mechanism. She heard a sudden creak in the floorboards to her left. A white woman emerged in her peripheral vision. Her skin was like milk glass and her hair flowed red from her scalp like blood from a wound. Her limbs were thin and fragile like those of a porcelain ballerina. Her lips began to part, in preparation to smile or talk. What happened next was horrifying. The woman's jaw contorted and unhinged, revealing a set of teeth, black with decay. The black tar dripped from her mouth, creating a waterfall of slime that spilled grotesquely over her bottom lip.

The can of half opened tuna clattered to the ground, spraying flakes of fish all over the floor. Blake's breath caught painfully in her chest. Reflexively, she bent down to pick up the can of tuna. When she lifted her head, the woman was gone. She wheezed and gasped straining her neck this way and that, searching for whatever it was she thought she saw.

"There's nothing there." She sighed and shakily took a seat. "I must be tired," she concluded. "God! I must really be tired." Her heart still pounding, she cleaned the tuna from the floor and carried on preparing her dinner. Her nerves forced her to have a second cigarette. Blake told herself it was understandable to be a little jumpy after making a big change. Plenty of people experienced odd sightings and nightmares due to nerves... didn't they?

Before calling it a night, Blake managed to strip the wallpaper from one wall of the kitchen and had started work stripping the paper surrounding the cupboards. Tomorrow, she planned on alternating between painting and stripping the walls. First and foremost, however, she needed a good night's sleep.

Chapter Four

At long last, Blake got her full eight hours of rest. She'd installed the headboard of her bed, along with the blackout curtains, before going to bed. Her day turned out to be very productive. She spent the late morning unpacking the remainder of her clothes and the rest of the day stripping and painting the kitchen walls. By the time the late afternoon had rolled around, Blake had finished painting the entire kitchen. Now, all she needed to do was paint the dining set and add a few charming art pieces to the wall, and the kitchen would be complete.

She stepped from the shower, having washed the day's sweat and dirt from her body, and gazed upon her heap of yellow stained clothing. Thankfully, she'd chosen to paint wearing a T-shirt and shorts she didn't particularly care too much for. Even so, she wondered how she would remove the paint stains.

"You've got bigger fish to fry, Blake!" she told herself. *"Don't worry about some silly paint stains. Besides, you've got lots of other paint projects to complete. Now you've got some designated paint clothes."*

Blake was proud of herself for finishing the kitchen. Feeling in the mood for celebration, she decided to open the bottle of wine she'd purchased from the liquor store during her trip to Providence. She navigated the kitchen gingerly, taking special care not to touch the freshly painted walls. The plastic protector crinkled beneath her feet. She didn't like the way it clung to her bare feet as she walked, nor did she enjoy inhaling the fumes from the paint. She, therefore, decided her wine would be best enjoyed on the patio.

It was only when she got out onto the patio that she realized: she didn't own any patio furniture. She dragged a chair from the kitchen table out onto the patio and sat down for a well-deserved glass of wine and a cigarette.

The air was chilly, but certainly not as cold as it had been. Blake ran a brush through her damp hair. The sun peaked out from behind the clouds, low in the horizon, and the forest buzzed with the activity of the evening critters. Blake sipped on her red wine and relaxed. The red embers of her cigarette blazed as she drew the smoke into her lungs. A warm, comforting sensation began in her head and spread throughout her body. She felt accomplished and at peace. It wasn't long until she began to drift off.

"Please don't leave me," a voice resonated eerily in the back of her head. Blake stirred. She felt fingers tugging at the skin on her neck. They were gentle at first, stroking up and down her neck and along the line of her jaw. Then, a pair of arms wrapped around her body, embracing her fiercely.

"I love you. Please don't leave me!" the voice begged. Blake jumped from the chair in panic. She fled the porch, tripping down the stairs and stumbling through the thick grass. She tore at herself in attempts to rid her body of whatever presence had taken hold of her. Her wet hair blinded her as she thrashed in fear.

"Get off of me! Get off of me! Get off of me!" she screamed. The apex of her shoe caught beneath a protruding tree root as she ran, causing her to hit the ground hard. She rolled over, her breath ragged in her chest. Where was the mysterious attacker? She stood and surveyed the property. There was no one in sight. Had she drifted off enough to have a nightmare? Was the ghostly figure simply a product of her imagination?

"God, I hope I'm drunk!" Blake thought. It was doubtful. One glass of wine wouldn't have caused such a realistic hallucination. Terrified, Blake walked slowly back to the house. She found her cigarette extinguished by the door. She picked it up and relit it, smoking it as fast as she could. Blake flung the butt onto the gravel path and hurried inside, locking the door behind her. She licked her lips and forced herself to take a deep breath in and out.

"It was just a dream," she stated firmly. Her phone then blared adamantly in her coat pocket.

Blake yelped, startled. Realizing it was just her ringtone, she reached into her pocket and answered her phone, doing her best to steady her voice.

"Hello?"

"Hi, Blake. This is Marlow Bannting from Bannting Funeral Home. I hope I haven't caught you at a bad time." Marlow was Blake's new employer.

"N-no, not at all," Blake stuttered.

"Great! Listen, I was thinking the other day and realized I have an apartment above the funeral home currently available for rent. I'm not sure if you've found a suitable place here in Providence, or not, but I thought I should call you to let you know I'd be pleased to offer you the apartment."

"Oh." Blake hesitated. "I-uh-I've actually found a place already."

"I see," Marlow responded. "Well, I suppose I should let you get settled in. I look forward to working with you soon."

The phone line went dead. Part of Blake wanted the man to keep talking. She felt very much alone and vulnerable.

"Come on, Blake, get yourself together!" She exhaled sharply. *"You're an independent woman! There is no one living in this house except for you!"* Blake marched herself into the kitchen to cook dinner. The paint fumes hit her, and she immediately turned in the other direction. It probably wasn't a great idea to prepare or eat dinner in a toxic smelling environment.

"Pizza and beer it is!" she declared, grabbing her keys from the counter.

Chapter Five

That morning, Blake's spirit was immediately heightened as soon as she entered her newly painted kitchen. The yellow paint had been a good choice. She now faced the task of cleaning up the kitchen. The plastic floor protector was still covering the ground. Bits of dried wallpaper lay dead on the plastic. She also had to go through the cupboards and clean out any old tins of soup.

Blake rolled up her sleeves and began gathering up the plastic and flakes of wallpaper from the ground. She had a garbage bag folded over the back of a chair, ready for collection. The plastic protector she could save for another project. The paper, on the other hand, had to go.

As Blake worked, she felt a chill circulate the room. It felt as though a window was open. Blake had cracked the window to allow for the paint fumes to defuse, but, she was certain she'd closed it. Sure enough, Blake went over to the window to find it sealed shut. A panic surfaced in her chest.

"Calm down, Blake. Old houses have drafts. There's absolutely nothing strange about a draft." Managing to suppress her nerves, Blake opened the cupboards and began extracting the many cans of expired chicken noodle soup. After removing the tenth can, Blake swore and threw up her hands in exasperation.

"Why on earth would someone keep this many cans of chicken noodle soup!" she exclaimed. Moreover, why didn't the realtor, or someone, clean the cupboards out before she moved in?

The soup was all from 1914, same as the scotch broth she'd initially found. Blake was starting to get the impression that whoever lived at the Harper House during that time period was a serious recluse!

Blake shrugged her shoulders. "Or, maybe someone just really liked chicken noodle soup," she surmised.

Blake, however, did not like chicken noodle soup, at least not the kind manufactured in a factory. Factory made chicken noodle soup was excruciatingly salty. The noodles were a soggy mess, and the chicken pieces reminded Blake of something she would feed a wild animal.

"This soup is going where it belongs: the trash!" Blake declared. She bundled the cans of soup in her arms and dumped them into the garbage bag.

A thought occurred to Blake just then: what sort of old crap would she find in the cellar?

Curious, Blake abandoned her task of cleaning the kitchen to take a peak. A cellar would presumably provide a great amount of storage. She opened the door to reveal a dark and narrow staircase. Above her was a metal chain. Upon pulling it, a light bulb illuminated the stairwell. The steps were cold concrete and coated in dust.

"Aw, man!" Blake groaned. There were probably all sorts of creepy crawlers living in the cellar. Blake wrapped her arms around her. The air had gone from cold to freezing. Clearly there was little to no insulation in the cellar, though, Blake didn't think it was even this cold outside. She flicked a switch at the bottom of the stairs. The cellar was a dank and unpleasant space. Cobwebs hung from the ceiling—a macabre decoration. A number of wooden shelving units stood flush with the walls. They appeared to be occupied with a number of empty glass bottles. Blake shivered and inched toward one of the shelves to take a closer look. She took a bottle from the shelf, wiping the label free of grime.

"Glo-Tone. Arterial solu—wait..." Blake paused, puzzled by what the label read. "Arterial solution. A cosmetic fluid?!" It couldn't be. The bottles on the shelves were empty bottles of embalming fluid. Blake frantically inspected each bottle. Some were disinfectants, some humectants, water softeners, cavity fluid, cauterizing agents, tints… they were all fluids used for embalming.

"Oh my God," Blake uttered in shock. She picked up an empty bottle of rose-scented humectant. How could this be?! Blake used the exact same humectant when she embalmed. What was it doing in the basement of the Harper House?!

A sense of dread welled up inside Blake. The bottles dated back to the early 1900s, just as the soup cans did. Why would anyone need so many bottles of embalming fluid? A blast of cold air hit Blake suddenly from behind. Chills went down her spine. Frightened, she quickly escalated the stairs, slamming the door at the top.

She took a moment to catch her breath. Blake didn't know what to do next. Should she tell someone about the bottles? Who would she tell? She wandered back to the kitchen with the intention of finishing up her cleaning, but what she saw on the kitchen counter stopped her dead in her tracks. The rusty cans of chicken noodle soup were on the counter, lined up neatly in rows.

"I—I thought I threw those out," Blake whispered. She peered into the garbage bag. No cans of soup. Blake knew for a fact she'd thrown the soup out. So… how did the cans magically end up back on the counter? Blake's fear was becoming unmanageable. There was only one explanation for the cans: someone or something dug them out of the trash and placed them on the counter.

Chapter Six

Blake's fingers trembled as she pulled a cigarette from its box. After the bizarre reappearance of the soup cans, she needed to get out of the house. She *must* have forgotten to throw them away. There couldn't be something or someone living in her house. Although… the memory of the man embracing Blake on the porch returned. She shuddered. She was currently standing on the porch, nervously smoking and drinking lemonade. The sun was out, the sky was blue, and the birds were twittering and jumping joyously from branch to branch. Had Blake not been so shaken by the events of the last few days, she'd be enjoying the afternoon.

She downed the last of her lemonade and dropped her finished cigarette butt into the cup.

"I guess from now on that cup will be my designated ash tray," she thought. She also thought it would be a good idea to go for a walk. It was universally known amongst psychologists that going for a walk improved one's mood. *"Pretty soon I'm going to need a psychologist!"* Blake couldn't help but wonder if the strange events she was experiencing were all in her head. *"A little fresh air will set me right,"* she thought. Ironically, she thought this while lighting another cigarette.

Blake walked down the convoluted dirt road, toward Providence. She tried to take her mind off of the Harper House by focusing on pleasant things such as the warmth of the sun and the harmonic sounds of the forest, but her attempts were to no avail. She couldn't stop wondering about the house's history. Who had lived in that house before her?

Blake sighed, exasperated. No matter how hard she tried, she couldn't enjoy the serenity of the woods. She paused for a moment to light her third cigarette of the day. The cigarette protruding ridiculously from her mouth, Blake was just about to light it, when she heard a hissing sound. She turned to her right to see a curious looking raccoon bumble drunkenly out from behind a tree.

"Funny," Blake thought, removing the cigarette from between her lips, *"raccoons are supposed to be nocturnal."*

The raccoon snarled, revealing a set of tiny sharp canines. Foam dripped from its mouth. A mad look shone wildly in the raccoon's beady eyes. Blake inched backward. The raccoon looked as though it was about to attack. It waved its behind in the air and anchored its human-like hands into the dirt, ready to pounce.

"Oh, God, no!" Blake screamed as the raccoon catapulted itself upwards like a spring. She threw her hands up to protect her face and was suddenly deafened by a thundering BOOM! Blake opened her eyes to find the raccoon belly up and bleeding on the road.

"Rabies," a voice stated. Blake startled and spun around. She watched in awe as an elderly woman swung down from a tree branch and dropped to the ground. She had a rifle slung over her shoulder as casual as a purse. "It's not uncommon for raccoons around these parts to get infected with rabies," the woman explained. "The disease makes them nasty. It didn't get you, did it?"

Blake shook her head. "Uh, no. It didn't." Blake was flabbergasted. Did this seventy-something-year-old woman just save her from a man eating raccoon?!

The woman introduced herself as Mary and bent down to pick up Blake's cigarette. "I think you dropped this," she said, handing it back. "Believe it or not, those things are probably more dangerous than a rabid raccoon," she added.

"Thanks," Blake said. "I mean, not for returning the cigarette. I'm trying to stop, anyway. I mean to say, thanks for—"

"Don't mention it, kid," Mary interrupted. She turned to leave.

"I—uh—I'm your new neighbor. My name's Blake," Blake called after her. "I met your grandson, Clyde. He works at the restaurant in town."

Mary stopped dead in her tracks and turned to face Blake. She had azure blue eyes. Blake could see she had once been very beautiful. "You moved into the Harper House, then?"

"Yes, I did," Blake answered.

Mary laughed, shook her head, and continued on her way. "You'll be out of there faster than a bat out of hell!" Mary scoffed under her breath.

"Sorry, what?" Mary inched her way down a shallow ravine and disappeared into the forest. "Wait!" Blake shouted. "What's wrong with the Harper House!" A number of crows cawed and fluttered from the trees. "You've got to be kidding me!" Blake groaned. The last thing she wanted to do was turn around and go back to the Harper House. Unfortunately, she didn't have much of a choice. She couldn't sleep in the forest. Who knew what sort of rabid rodents were dwelling in the woods. At least the Harper House provided protection from the outside world. What it didn't protect against, however, was whatever it was that dwelled inside. Marlow Bannting's apartment offer was looking more and more appealing to Blake.

Blake returned to the house just as the sun was beginning to creep behind the horizon. Upon her arrival, she immediately turned on all the lights in the house. She felt like a little girl for doing so, but having the lights on comforted her. She hurried up to the bathroom on the second floor and ran a bath. Surely a soothing bubble bath would relax her enough to fall asleep. A bottle of wine wouldn't hurt, either.

The warm water and soapy fragrance paired with the alcohol made Blake's eyelids heavy and sent her head swimming.

"Works like a charm," she said, hiccupping. An hour of drunken bathing passed before Blake managed to drag herself from the comforting confines of the tub's walls. "Time for sleep," she slurred, wrapping herself clumsily in a towel. Too tipsy to remember to drain the tub, Blake stumbled into her bedroom, leaving a trail of drips behind her. Her body still damp, she climbed into bed, bundling the blankets firmly about her chin. She passed out almost instantly. That night, Blake would experience more than just a drunken nightmare.

Chapter Seven

Blake's sleep was chaotic. Her inebriated mind drifted in and out of consciousness. She tossed and turned, sending the blankets and pillows all over her room. The atmosphere registered as unsettled. Somebody was there, watching her frenzied slumber. He liked watching her sleep. In fact, it made him hungry. Blake knew this. She wanted to get away, but her mind was entrapped—frozen in the land of nightmares.

He took his mount of the bed, his eyes fixed on Blake's every movement. His breath was loud and hot. Blake could feel his heart beating against her own. She felt his fingernails raking her scalp, his lips brushing against her cheek, and his legs clench firmly around her pelvis. She struggled and sobbed beneath the weight of his body.

"GET AWAY FROM ME!" she shrieked, thrusting her fists toward the man. She kicked and thrashed until the weight lifted from her body. Gasping, Blake opened her eyes to an empty room. Although the room was vacant of anyone other than herself, Blake distinctly heard the sound of a man crying. Terrified, she threw herself from the bed and bolted to the door. Realizing she was still naked from her bath, Blake hurriedly grabbed her housecoat from the hook in the bathroom, flung it over her exposed body, and swooped down the stairs. She wanted to get as far away from her room as possible.

The early morning air was crisp, and the grass glistened with dew. Blake liked the way it chilled her bare feet. She was smoking, again. She scarcely knew what else to do.

"Oh, God!" she moaned, crouching close to the earth. She could see ants and beetles crawling about, minding their own business. Blake almost wished she was an insect. Did insects feel fear? Blake was tired of being scared. She wanted answers.

There was a rustling amidst the foliage behind Blake just then. She turned to spot a chipmunk darting and weaving through the grass. Blake was reminded of the rabid raccoon she'd stumbled upon the other day.

"Hang on a second," Blake recalled, *"Mary knows something about this place."* While Blake had been having breakfast at the restaurant, Clyde had said: *'The Harper House? Isn't that the place where they found the…'* He then referred to Mary as a 'bit of a character.' Mary

also made a snide remark implying that something was awry with the Harper House.

"Oh, something's awry alright!" Blake declared, standing straight. Blake had questions for Mary. Whether Mary liked it or not, Blake was going to pay her a visit… right after she put on some clothes.

 Fully clothed and determined, Blake steered her jeep down the treacherous dirt road, on her way to see her neighbor. It was 7 am, and Blake didn't particularly care if Mary was a morning person or not.

"You'll be out of there quicker than a bat out of hell!" Mary's words echoed over and over in Blake's head. Was the Harper House haunted? Blake needed to know.

Mary's house was similar in stature to the Harper House. It, however, gave off more of a rustic ambiance. The house was constructed of a lightly stained wood. Wind chimes and glass mobiles dangled from the trees in Mary's yard. As they danced in the wind, they produced a melancholic song.

Blake parked her jeep hastily along the side of the road and rushed over to Mary's front door. She wrapped her knuckles frantically on the door and waited, tapping her foot incessantly. Footsteps creaked behind the door. Mary emerged.

"What do you want?" she said, gruffly. She was wearing a set of fleece pajamas. Clearly, she wasn't a morning person.

"I need to talk to you about the Harper House," Blake answered. "It's urgent! I think the place is haunted."

"Haunted, eh?" Mary cocked an eyebrow. She gestured for Blake to come inside.

The interior of Mary's house was surprisingly ordinary, save for the taxidermy.

"What are you gawking at!?" Mary barked. "Haven't you ever seen a stuffed deer head before?"

"Uh, no, actually," Blake responded. She took a seat on a couch coated in floral upholstery. Mary took the armchair across from her.

"So," Mary began, "What exactly has been going on in the Harper House?"

Blake described the frightening events that had occurred to her. She told Mary about the perverted male presence and the disfigured woman. She told Mary about the embalming fluids she found, the lingering rose scent, and the mysterious reappearing soup cans. By the time Blake was finished talking, she was winded and blue in the face.

Mary didn't seem one bit phased by Blake's stories. "You haven't eaten, have you?" she asked.

"No, I guess I haven't," Blake admitted. Her stomach grumbled as if on cue.

"Good. I'm making steak and eggs. I've got oranges in the fridge. You're going to sit down and join me."

Having been left no choice, Blake followed Mary to her kitchen. She appeared to be an avid cook given the number of cooking instruments that hung from the walls. Mary pushed a large brass bowl filled with fruit toward Blake. Blake helped herself to an apple.

"Do you drink coffee?" Mary inquired. She removed a tin of coffee grounds from her cupboard.

"Yes, I do."

Chapter Eight

Blake sat quietly munching her apple while Mary worked in the kitchen. Despite her age and elderly appearance, Mary was agile. Her nimble hands worked quickly. The steak and eggs sizzled on the skillet. The succulent smell had Blake's mouth watering.

"So," Mary said, dishing the steak and eggs onto two plates, "I suppose you've come to the conclusion that the Harper House is haunted, is that right?"

"I'm not sure," Blake answered. "I don't know if—"

"Let me guess, you don't know if the house is haunted or if you're just going bonkers," Mary finished.

"Exactly."

Mary brought the breakfast over to the table. She served Blake and then sat across from her. "You're not going crazy," she said, "The Harper House is most definitely haunted."

Blake stared at her eggs for a moment. She was half relieved yet half shocked by the news. On one hand, she wasn't totally barking mad, on the other, her new house sheltered ghosts.

"This house used to belong to my grandmother," Mary stated. "I inherited it when she passed away. As a child, she warned me never to visit the Harper House. But, being the defiant little bugger that I was, I didn't listen. I wandered over there one day and saw something that both perplexed and frightened me. I saw the silhouette of a man holding a bag. The man was terribly thin and lumbered along his driveway as though he was about to fall over. Whatever was in that bag clinked as he walked. I hurried back to my grandmother and told her what I had seen. She chagrined me and told me the story of the Harper House."

Mary paused then to take a bite of her steak. "What was the story?" Blake probed, impatiently.

"Just a minute!" Mary declared. "I'm hungry!" She took a few more bites before continuing.

"The man I saw was the ghost of Wyatt Harper. He was a disturbed old man with a tragic past. His mother and father were killed by a mad horse, and his wife, Mabel, died during childbirth. The child was lost as well. Suffice to say, the grief turned Wyatt's mind. He worked briefly as an undertaker in the city of Providence. He, however, gave up the practice to be with his pregnant wife. After her death, many citizens, including my grandmother, would see Wyatt hanging around the mortuary supply shop. He'd go in carrying an empty leather bag and exit gingerly, struggling with the weight of the bag. Nobody knew what he was using the preservatives for… until one day when my grandmother went for a walk by the Harper House and smelled a ghastly scent traveling on the wind. She alerted the police, suspecting someone or something had died on the property. What the police found was abhorred. The bodies of Wyatt and his wife— who died years before him— were rotting together in the bedroom, locked in an eternal embrace."

Chapter Nine

"Hang on a minute," Blake said, having finished her last bite of steak. "Wyatt's wife was in the bed with him? Do you mean to say—"

Mary nodded. "Wyatt never buried his wife. He lost his mind after her death. Instead of holding a funeral ceremony and moving on with his life, he continuously embalmed Mabel. I care not to think about what he did with her body."

Blake shuddered. Wyatt's spirit must have mistook Blake for Mabel. That's why she'd feel him caressing her in her sleep. The deformed woman Blake saw in her kitchen must have been Mabel.

"What am I supposed to do now?" Blake asked, rubbing her face, wearily. "I can't live in a house with a pair of ghosts!"

"No," Mary agreed. "You most certainly cannot! Anyone who's ever attempted to live there has been chased out by the Harper spirits, or worse. I don't know why that godforsaken place is even still up on the market. It must be dirt cheap."

Mary's supposition was right. The down payment Blake made on the house was very reasonable. Blake assumed it was due to the house's isolated location and somewhat downtrodden state. Little had she known it was because of the house's macabre history.

"I suggest getting out of there as fast as you can," Mary said. "Get a hotel, call a friend, live with a relative… just get out while you still can! If you ask me, that house has imprisoned the souls of the Harpers. You don't want to be next!"

Before leaving Mary's house, Blake thanked her for her food and for her help. She was descending down the steps of the house, when Mary stopped her.

"One more thing before you leave." she said. "Do you happen to have fire insurance?"

"Uh, yes," Blake responded, baffled by the question. "The realtor recommended it due to the house's location in the forest, where fires sometimes occur during the dry season."

"Good," Mary said. She wished Blake good luck and disappeared back into her house.

As soon as Blake had reception, she called Marlow Bannting from Bannting Funeral Home.

"Hello, this is Marlow Bannting speaking," Marlow answered, professionally.

"Hi, Marlow, it's Blake. I'm calling because something has come up with my current housing situation. I've suddenly found myself in need of a new location to live. Is your apartment still available?" Blake held her breath. If Marlow had rented his apartment, Blake was screwed.

"Of course it is!" Marlow beamed.

Blake sighed in relief. "That's excellent news. Would I be able to move in as soon as today? I know it seems sudden, but my situation is desperate."

"I don't see why not," Marlow responded. "I'm at the funeral home late tonight, anyhow. Forgive my probing, but, where exactly is it that you're currently staying?"

Blake hesitated. She didn't particularly want to mention the house being haunted. "I was situated about a half hour outside of Providence in an old Victorian house. Things, um, didn't quite work out."

"Victorian house, you say? Is that, by chance, the Harper House you're referring to?" Marlow inquired.

"Yes!" Blake answered, astonished. "How did you know?"

Marlow chuckled. "Let's just say, I've done a few too many removals from that place. People die there all the time. It's a real shame. I don't know what it is. Some say the place is cursed, but I'm not sure I believe in all that mumbo jumbo. Anyway, perhaps it's best that things didn't work out for you there. I think you'll love the apartment. It's really quite lovely."

Blake swallowed. She hadn't realized so many people had died at the Harper House. "Is the place already furnished?" she asked. Regardless of the answer, Blake wasn't willing to spend the time disassembling her bed. She'd take her necessities and leave.

"Yes, it is. I probably should have mentioned that. You've got my number, so if you need any help, just let me know." Marlow said good-bye and hung up.

Over the course of the rest of the day, Blake frantically packed up her belongings and hightailed it to Bannting Funeral Home. By dinner time, she was in her new apartment, safe and sound from the ghosts of Mabel and Wyatt Harper.

Two Weeks Later

It was Blake's second day on the job as prep room manager at Bannting Funeral Home. Blake was feeling positive about her new role and was proud of herself for the number of days she'd gone without putting a cigarette in her mouth.

"Blake, check this out." Marlow entered the break room where Blake was having her lunch. He slapped a newspaper down in front of her. The headline read: Harper House Mysteriously Burns to the Ground.

"Looks like someone will be getting a rather fat check from the insurance company!" Marlow remarked.

The fire was no mystery to Blake. One name came to mind: Mary.

The End

More Books by Carrie Bates:

The Haunting of Thomas House

The Haunting of Maple Mansion

The Haunting of Hilltop Mansion

The Haunting of Whitfield Mansion

The Haunting of Owensboro Mansion

The Haunting of Maynard Mansion

The Haunting of Kessinger Mansion

The Haunting of Krakow Convent

The Haunting of St. Doyle Seminary

Printed in Poland
by Amazon Fulfillment
Poland Sp. z o.o., Wrocław